British Library Cataloguing in Publication Data

A catalogue record for this book is available
from the British Library

ISBN 0 340 58632 X

Text and illustrations copyright © Mick Inkpen 1989

The right of Mick Inkpen to be identified as the author
of this work has been asserted by him in accordance
with the Copyright, Design and Patents Act 1988

First published 1989
This edition first published 1993

Published by Hodder and Stoughton Children's Books,
a division of Hodder and Stoughton Ltd,
Mill Road, Dunton Green, Sevenoaks, Kent TN13 2YA

Printed in Italy by L.E.G.O., Vicenza

The Blue Balloon

Mick Inkpen

HODDER AND STOUGHTON
LONDON SYDNEY AUCKLAND

The day after my birthday party Kipper found a soggy blue balloon in the garden.
Which was odd because the balloons at my party were red and white.
I blew it up.

At first I thought it was just
an ordinary balloon. But now I am
not so sure.

It is shiny and squeaky and
you can make rude noises with it.
And if you give it a rub you can
stick it on the ceiling.
Just like an ordinary balloon.

But there is something odd about my balloon.

It doesn't matter how much you blow it up, it just goes on getting bigger...

and bigger until...

You see it never ever bursts. Never ever.

I have squeezed it...   squashed it...

...and whacked it with a stick.

-e-e-e-e-e-e-e-e-e-e-e-e-e-e-e-etched it!

I have kicked it...

run it over...

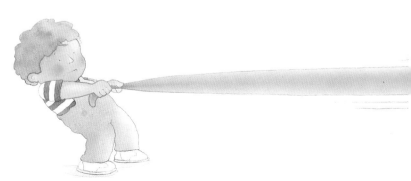

...and stre-e-e-e-e-e-e-e-e-e-e-e-e

And Kipper has attacked it.
But it is Indestructible.

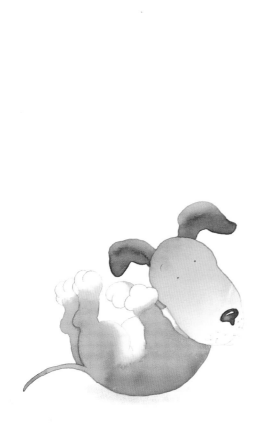

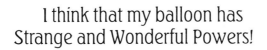

I think that my balloon has
Strange and Wonderful Powers!

The other day it disappeared completely...

...and when it came back it was square!

And this morning, while I was taking it for a walk…

and up ...   Oops!

It took me up . . . and up . . .

... it decided to take me for a fly!

And finally ...

...down.

It was quite a trip, but we were back in time for tea.

So if you find a soggy old balloon...

Whatever you do don't throw it away.

Especially if it's a blue one.

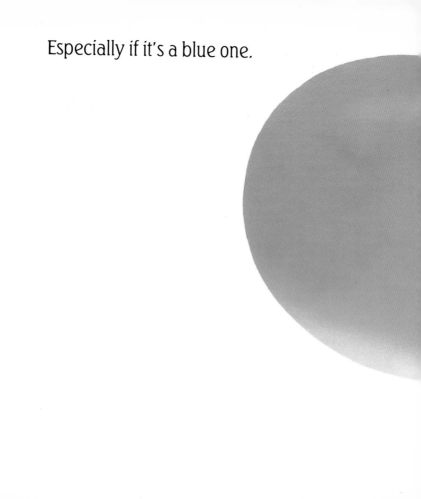

You never know what it will do next.

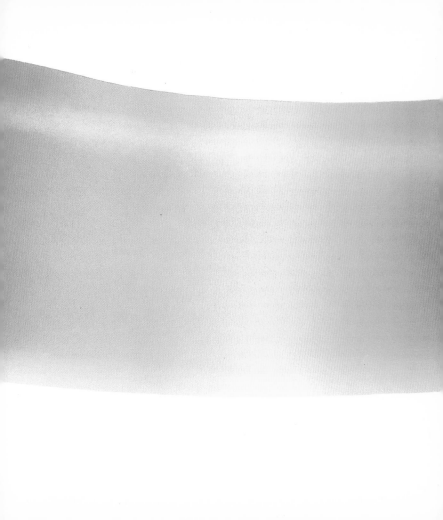